That One Summer

LIA & ZACH'S ORIGIN STORY

TUCKAWAY BAY

MADELEINE JAIMES

SAND DUNE BOOKS

That One Summer

A Tuckaway Bay Origin Story: Lia & Zach

Maddie James writing as
Madeleine Jaimes

Sand Dune Books by Maddie James

www.maddiejamesbooks.com

Copyright © 2020 Madeleine Jaimes

All rights reserved. The unauthorized reproduction or distribution of this copyrighted work, in whole or part, by any electronic, mechanical, or other means, is illegal and forbidden.

Author: Jaimes, Madeleine

Title: That One Summer / Madeleine Jaimes

Description: First edition. Sand Dune Books

Subjects: Fiction / Women's Fiction | Friendships | Relationships| Beach | Young Love

Editor: Wendee Mullikin, Purple Pen Wordsmithing, LLC

Cover Design by Author Journey Solutions and DALL-E

This is a work of fiction. Characters, settings, names, occurrences, and story elements are a product of the author's imagination and bear no resemblance to any actual person, living or dead, places or settings, and/or other occurrences. Any incidences of resemblance are purely coincidental.

Published by Turquoise Morning, LLC., dba Jacobs Ink, LLC.

PO Box 20, New Holland, OH 43145.

Learn more about Madeleine Jaimes at www.maddiejamesbooks.com

Join the VIP Newsletter List at Newsletter – Maddie James Books

Praise For Maddie James

No other author can hold a candle to Maddie James in the short story department ... Not hard to fall in love with perfection. ~ Isha Coleman, Candid Book Reviews

All of My Heart *will have you up, down, hot and cold, and maybe just a little bit desperate too!* ~ Lamplight Review & Promotion on Goodreads

Heartwarming and tender... [Falling for Grace] will brighten many dreary afternoons in small town America... [James] shows special talent for traditional romance. ~ Affair de Coeur Reviews

Captured my attention from the beginning. It had me in laughter and tears.... ~ JoAnne, Romancing the Book Reviews

I absolutely loved this book...loved...loved...loved. I craved a sweet lighthearted book that would touch my heart, and this was perfect, just perfect.
~ Kris, Goodreads

This book had the sweetest proposal I have ever come across in my life. I actually cried.
~ Shay, Goodreads

Just one more page, just one more page, okay, just one more page... ~ Amazon Review

Loved this book so much I've read it multiple times! ~ Amazon Review

A great story combined with strong characterization and perfect pacing...Brava Ms. James. I loved this story. ~ Amazon Vine Voice Review

That One Summer

Lia Langston thinks she's heading to the beach for one last summer fling with her girlfriends before jumping into the working world of Corporate America. She has a plan. One week with her five girlfriends, then a summer job at the cute dress shop at the beach mall.

That last part doesn't happen.

Before she knows it, she is swept off her feet by a local guy named Zach and whisked into a summer job managing the front office of his Aunt Grace's beach motel.

Summer flies. She and Zach fall in love. And come August, Aunt Grace offers her a permanent, full-time position. Zach is thrilled, of course, because he wants Lia *permanently* in his life.

But that summer was only meant to be her last hurrah. Corporate America is waiting back in Chicago and Lia must choose. Can she have her beach life and Zach, and an exciting corporate job, too?

One

Summer 2001, June

ZACH ALLEN DOWNSHIFTED THE OLD pickup truck and squinted, looking down the road. The sun was wicked this morning, slanting in off the ocean and reflecting the asphalt, but he could see someone pulled off to the side. He hoped they didn't need help—he was running late as it was, and Aunt Grace never cut him any slack being late to work—but he also knew he would never leave anyone stranded on this road.

Lucky for him, this narrow stretch of Old Beach Road was not well-traveled since the Tuckaway Bay bypass went in about ten years ago, so he didn't have to worry about approaching vehicles and the glinting sun, as he maneuvered around the parked car.

Not lucky for the person, though, because if they were having car trouble, pulling off onto that sand probably was not the best idea. Tourist, he figured.

A small red sports car came into focus as he slowed and approached. He saw someone exit the vehicle. A young woman went to the front of the car, bent to look at the driver's side front tire, stood again, and then kicked it. Retreating to the rear, she pushed her key fob to pop the trunk lid and pulled out two pieces of luggage, setting them aside. Ducking back into the trunk, she poked around and tugged at something.

Zach downshifted once more and braked, put on his emergency flashers, and parked slightly to the left of the car, but still on the asphalt.

The woman looked his way, her long brunette hair a shimmering wave in the morning sun as she turned. She looked to be about his age, he guessed. He contemplated briefly savoring her quick glance, studying her pert nose and her plump pink lips and her light brown eyes, then thought better of it. She needed a hand, which he would gladly lend, and then he'd get to work.

He got out of the truck.

She side-stepped and moved closer. When she did, he got a good look at the back of the car—some sort of brand-spanking new Honda roadster, it seemed. Illinois plates.

Just as he thought. Tourist. Or worse yet, summer help.

"Hi. Do you have a cell phone that works out here?" she asked.

Her face held all kinds of expectation, and he hated to dash her hopes, but it couldn't be helped. Zach took a few steps her way and shoved his hands into his pockets. "Naw. It's spotty out here. You'll be lucky to get much of a signal until you get closer to town."

"Oh." She glanced back at the car. "I may have picked up a nail."

Zach leaned left to look at the flat tire, then back to her, catching her eye again. Hazel. Her eyes were hazel, not light brown. "Maybe."

"I think I have a jack. And one of those donut tire things. Are you headed into town?" She crossed her arms over her chest and studied him. "If you don't mind, could you go to a gas station and see if a wrecker could come back out here to help me? I hate to ask."

"No."

"No? No, what?"

"No, I'm not going to town, and no, I can't find someone to help you."

Her hands dropped to her sides and she exhaled, eyes flashing wide. "Well, could you give me a ride then, so I could use a phone? Or a spot where my cell will work? I'll pay you."

He shook his head. "Can't do that either. Company policy."

Her face screwed up. "What?"

Ticking his head toward the pickup, he said, "The boss doesn't like it when I pick up girls on the road."

"So, you pick up girls often?"

He grinned. "Never."

"Then why...."

Zach couldn't hold back his laughter any longer and suddenly gave loose. The woman just stood staring at him.

"I don't see what's so funny."

"Just getting your goat."

"My...goat?"

"Yeah. Teasing you. Funny, huh?"

Again, she heaved another sigh. "Not really. Thanks for stopping. I guess I'll figure out a Plan B." Turning, she picked up her two bags and tossed them back into the trunk, slamming the lid. She headed for the driver's side seat—not looking at him—and reached for her keys and purse. He'd let this go on long enough.

"So, what are you going to do? Walk?"

She faced him. "Yes."

"I don't think so."

Her right brow arched. "Oh? I'm perfectly capable."

"I'm sure you are." He shifted his stance. "Hey, look. I was kidding. Sorry. Local humor.

But I guess you aren't from around here, so maybe it got lost on you. People are always getting stranded in the sand and cell phones never work. I can change the tire. Fully intended to all along, that's why I stopped. Pop that trunk back open."

The woman eyed him, warily. He supposed he deserved that. "You're sure?"

"Yes."

"All right. But first, what's your name?"

"Why?"

She angled closer, a smirky smile on her face. "Because when I call your employer and tell them what an ass you are, I want to make sure I get your name right."

"You know my boss?"

"Easy enough to find, seeing your employer's business is written on the side of your truck."

Zach decided right then and there that he liked this woman. She had spunk. He glanced back to his partially open truck door. *Sea Glass Inn at Tuckaway Bay* was clearly painted on the side. Yet, he already knew that. "Name's Zach Allen. And yours?"

She moved past him and popped the trunk again. "Lia Langston."

"Gonna be here for the week, Lia Langston?"

"No."

"Two weeks?"

She shook her head. "No, Zach Allen. I'm here for the summer."

While he rarely liked the idea of getting attached to summer help—they came, they left, they broke hearts—the idea that she would be around for a while made him grin.

"Where are you working?" Hell, he hoped it wasn't for Grace.

"At the Seaside Shoppes Mall, the dress shop."

Zach knew absolutely nothing about a dress shop. Good.

"Well, let me at it." He inched up to the trunk, then added, "You start work today?"

She shook her head. "No. I start next Monday. I just drove in from Chicago. Stayed in Elizabeth City last night. I'm meeting my girlfriends for the week at a beach rental called Tequila Sunrise. We came here about every break during college. You know it?

He knew the house. "North of the lighthouse, right? Beachfront."

"Yes."

"Nice place."

"Belongs to friends of a friend."

"Ah. I see. So, you're in school?"

She shook her head. "Just graduated. ECU. I may do graduate school back in Chicago next year. Not sure."

Zach studied her. That bit of information was interesting. From dress shop to graduate school? Not your typical summer help. "I see. Well, this tire isn't going to change itself."

"What can I do?"

Just stand there and look pretty. Zach realized the second that thought exited his brain how sexist it sounded. Fortunately, he hadn't said it out loud. But it was what he thought, and she *was* pretty, even though their brief conversation led him to believe there was a whole lot more to her than pretty. "Naw. It won't take me long."

"Thanks, Zach Allen. I sure appreciate it."

LATER THAT AFTERNOON, LIA SHARED the story with three of her girlfriends. Lined up on the deck of Tequila Sunrise, red cups at their fingertips filled with alcoholic beverages of choice, they lay soaking up rays.

"So, he changed my tire, and then he was on his way."

"Was he cute?" Her college roommate, Alice, leaned toward her.

Lia sidled her a glance. "Honestly, I think he was the most beautiful boy I've ever seen. Darkest blue eyes ever. Shaggy blond hair that definitely looked sun kissed. I wonder if he surfs or fishes?" She thought about that for a second. "Fishes. He didn't look like a surfer dude. He was tall, too. Broad chest. Long tan legs. He wore cargo shorts, a t-shirt, and deck shoes. I'd say he was about our age."

"Sounds yummy. Does he have a friend?"

Lia sat up and looked past Alice to Maggie. "Our conversation really didn't go that deep, Mags. We basically only talked about the tire and no cell service and college."

"Well, damn." Maggie reached for her drink. "He's a student? He knows people then. I'd like to find a guy to hang out with this week."

Lia rolled her eyes. "I don't know, Maggie, but you never seem to have difficulty finding men. They flock to you."

Maggie beamed, pulled her sunhat down over her head, and leaned back in the wooden Adirondack chair. "I like a good romp in the sheets once in a while, you know."

"We know," the two chorused.

Lia settled back into her chair, too. "He didn't say he was in college, so I don't know. But he works at the Inn, I guess, since he was driving one of their trucks. You know the one, down by the pier? Sea Glass Inn, I think."

"That's the one," Alice said. "The Inn is great. It has a huge multi-purpose room that people rent out for birthday parties and weddings. We used to go there all the time for stuff when I was growing up, especially in the off season. The locals use it more then. And, they have that private beach access that seems to go for miles."

Alice would know, Lia thought, because she is a local. Alice was the reason the six of them—Lia, Maggie, Alice, Julia, and identical twin sisters, Wren and Willow—started coming to Tuckaway Bay and renting Tequila Sunrise in the first place. "Maybe we can get friendly with Zach Allen and he'll give us beach access one of these days."

"I doubt it," Alice told her. "From what I understand, Grace Allen, who owns the property, keeps a tight, guests-only, no trespassing policy on the place."

"Oh well. It was a thought."

"Yeah."

Lia thought about Grace. "Did you say her last name is Allen? Do you suppose Zach is related to her?"

Alice shrugged. "Maybe. Grace is sort of an icon in Tuckaway Bay. Born and raised here, inherited the Inn property, and made it a booming business. She never married, I understand, but I believe she may have raised a nephew."

"Hm. That might be Zach?"

"Perhaps. I don't know."

Maggie leaned in. "Anyone know where the other girls went to?"

"Not sure, but if Julia is with them, Wren and Willow won't get into too much trouble." Alice shifted and moved her legs to the side of the chair.

"True. I hope Willow isn't out trying to score some pot."

Lia raised her head and shot Maggie a look. "Oh hell, she wouldn't."

"You never know with that one." Maggie shrugged.

Alice side-stepped over the end of Lia's deck chair and headed for the sliding glass door. "I'm going in. Just so you know, they went down to the Seaside Shoppes. I don't think Willow is going to get weed there."

"Also true," Lia said.

"And dibs on the shower."

"I'm next!"

"Go for it." That was fine with Lia. Alice and Maggie could go first, and then she'd shower before the others got back. For now, all she wanted was to sip her red cup margarita and have another moment alone with her thoughts, perhaps to contemplate the most beautiful boy ever who came to her rescue this morning.

THAT ONE SUMMER

A CROWD HAD GATHERED NEAR THE lighthouse, locals mostly, with a few weeklies thrown in. They called them weeklies—Zach and his friends—because every week there was a new crop of teenagers or college students who came for the family vacation and were dying to get away from their parents for an evening. They'd stay for a week, get to know everyone, and then leave.

It was cool most of the time. A week wasn't a long time to build much of a connection with anyone. The summer help... Now, that was where a guy could get into trouble.

Tonight, they'd built a bonfire, and the crowd was growing larger and rowdier than normal. Zach hoped it didn't get out of control. Summer kick-off, he guessed. The natives were restless.

Most of Zach's friends in Tuckaway Bay were local. They worked the fishing boats, bussed and waited tables, tended bar, or worked retail. That was about it. And for most of those jobs, relying on summer wages and tips was crucial to getting by during the winter. Zach's situation was different.

He didn't grow up in Tuckaway Bay, but was considered a local by everyone he knew. He had spent every summer there with Aunt Grace, his dad's oldest sister, since he was five years old. That was the year his mom died, and his dad didn't know what to do with him for summer vacation. Aunt Grace showed up on their New Hampshire doorstep early that summer and whisked him back to North Carolina. He didn't see his dad again until early September.

That pattern lasted for thirteen years until Zach went off to college. At that point, he made his way to Sea Glass Inn and back, on his own time and terms, but still worked for Grace every summer.

Tuckaway Bay was just as much his home as was the small town in New Hampshire. He'd learned to fish there—surf, sound, and on the boats. Played summer ball. Took swimming, golf, and surfing lessons. He'd also learned to be independent and take care of himself. Grace made sure he pulled his weight and took care of his own problems.

Generally, he hung out like all the other local beach bum kids—loving every minute. He'd return home in the fall for school, tan and fit, and catch the eyes of most girls up north.

Which he'd admit, was a bit of a turn-on for a squirrely teenage boy.

Aunt Grace became his substitute mom. His dad never remarried, so she was it for him. He'd forever be grateful. And he knew the feeling was mutual. Since middle school, he'd worked every summer full time. At first, it was odd jobs and cleaning up the grounds. She had a certain way she liked things to look every morning at the Inn. There were three beachfront buildings that made up the Inn, six cottages, the pool area and gazebo, and the private beach that spanned them all. Taking care of the grounds as a fourteen-year-old was a big job.

But he did it. And every year—from middle school through college graduation—he took on more jobs and learned different aspects of running the Inn. Now, with Grace getting older, so much of the responsibility fell to him, and he was happy to take it off her hands for a few months—tourist season, when they were the busiest. Aunt Grace did a lot of pointing and supervising, and he didn't mind one bit. He knew, however, that he had decisions to make soon—would he stay at the Inn and continue to work for his aunt? Or was it time to train someone else, so he could move on and put his MBA to good use, when he finished in six months?

Not something he had to decide tonight. He'd agonized over the decision for some time now. While he was itching to get started on a career, he felt almost heartsick at the thought of leaving Grace and Sea Glass Inn.

Pushing back from the fence he'd been leaning against, he glanced up the shore, toward the north, and gradually started walking that way. He wouldn't be missed, he knew that. Too many people. Besides, at about the halfway point between the lighthouse and the pier sat a beach house called Tequila Sunrise, and he wondered if he just might catch a glimpse of the summer help he'd run into earlier this morning.

Two

As it turned out, Willow found a weed man. She claimed she wasn't seeking it out—that the opportunity fell into her lap. Serendipity, she called it.

"And you keep telling yourself that, Willow, while you take another drag off that funny cigarette." Lia stood looking off the deck toward the horizon. The sun setting behind them cast an eerie, dusk-like glow over the beach. To the south, she could see a crowd gathering near the lighthouse, and smoke from a potential bonfire. "I didn't think bonfires were allowed on the beach here."

Alice leaned into the deck. "It's not June fifteenth yet. Tuckaway Bay allows bonfires up until then with a permit. Once tourist season kicks in, no bonfires anywhere, so the locals usually head down to the national seashore where its legal." She glanced down the beach.

"But I'm doubting those guys even bothered with a permit."

Willow sidled up against the deck rail. "Maybe we should walk down there."

"Oh, yes." Maggie joined them. "We could meet cute guys."

Willow shrugged. "I already met one today."

"We know, Willow, and you bought weed."

"He's stopping by later, after his shift."

Lia gave her the side-eye. "Seriously, Willow? You told your drug dealer where we are staying?"

"Why not?"

"Because, well... He's a drug dealer?"

"Chill, Lia. Pot isn't drugs. He was our waiter at the restaurant where we had lunch. He just graduated from ECU too. I thought I recognized him. He approached me as we were leaving."

"Well, that's what drug dealers do. Approach."

"It wasn't like that."

"Yeah, right."

Wren intercepted. "Actually, it wasn't, Lia. I think the guy overheard us talking as he stepped up to take our order."

"Fine. I believe you. Just like I believe Maggie doesn't seek out men for sexual favors."

"Oh, I definitely do that." Maggie piped up.

Lia rolled her eyes. *Am I the only sane person here?*

"You don't know what you are missing, Lia." Willow scooted up on the deck, sitting on the rail and looking over the side at the dunes. She sucked in another drag off the joint and brought both feet up and balanced herself there. "With weed, I mean." She exhaled, long.

Lia stood back. "I'm good," she told her. "Don't you freaking fall. You hear me?"

"Quit being such a mother hen."

Alice stepped up with a pitcher filled with a dark pink beverage. "Right. That's my job. Anyone need a refill?"

"What is that?"

"Fruit Punch ala Alice. Some juice, Kool-Aid, fruit, a whole lot of rum, gin, and probably tequila. I lost track."

"You're drinking? You usually don't."

"It's beach week. We have the house. No designated driver needed."

Alice always took on the role of DD. Lia was glad to see unwind a bit.

"True. Yum. I will take some of that." Lia put out her cup and glanced at Willow. "To each their own. I'd rather pickle my brain with alcohol than fry it with smoke."

Willow giggled. "Go right ahead, Lia. Your brain, your choice."

Julia stepped out onto the deck. "Can we

turn these string lights on? I think it would be cute."

"Sure."

Julia flipped the switch.

Maggie rushed up to her. "Oh, cute sundress! Did you get that today?"

She nodded. "Yes, at the dress shop where Lia will be working. Isn't it darling?

"It's super cute." Maggie made her twirl. "You look so pretty under the lights. Definitely boy bait."

Julia smirked. "Hell, Maggie. I'm not looking to be bait. Besides, Mark's back home pining away, waiting for me to give him an answer to his proposal."

"Well, don't keep him waiting forever, Julia. You've been stringing him along since high school."

Winking, Julia strolled away and wiggled her pinky finger. "Why not? Right now, he's wrapped firmly around this little finger of mine."

"Marriage, bah." Willow hopped down from the deck and glanced about. "Not for me and never will be." She glanced about. "Jesus, we're lit up like a fucking Christmas tree with these lights."

"Isn't that what we're going for? Now your drug dealer can easily find you." Lia laughed and tugged at Willow's hand. "Come take a walk with me." She led her toward the dune walkway.

Willow handed her joint off to her sister. "Keep that safe," she told her.

"Aye, aye, captain." Wren saluted.

The two strolled down the walkway and over the dune toward the beach in silence. "It's getting dark," Willow said.

"Yep."

"You okay, Lia?" They approached the stairs to the beach and took a couple of steps down.

She nodded. "Yes, I'm fine. I was just wondering how you're doing, though. With your dad passing a few weeks ago, I know it hasn't been easy on you. Wren too. And you've been getting high a lot more lately."

Willow stopped and put up a hand. "Lia, look. I'm coping. So is Wren. It's beach week. Give me that, okay? The real world awaits around the corner, and I need to let go for a while before that happens."

Their gazes danced over each other's for a moment. "Of course." Lia gave her a hug.

"Willow?"

The women pulled apart. Willow turned toward the male voice. "Fred?"

"Hey. I thought that was you. Want to take a walk? Maybe check out the bonfire?"

"Sure!"

Lia cleared her throat and touched Willow's arm.

"Oh. Fred, this is my friend Lia," Willow said. "Lia, this is Fred. My drug dealer."

"Willow!"

Fred laughed. "God don't let that get around. My mother would have a fit. I just know where to look if you need some more."

Smiling, Lia waved. "Hi Fred. Nice to meet you."

"Same."

Willow turned away from Lia then, tripped down the last two steps, and joined him. They headed down the beach. As Lia watched them walk away, her gaze shifted, and for the second time today, she saw the most beautiful boy in the world approaching her.

He grinned, shoving his hands into his cargo pants pockets.

Lia chuckled. "Well, hello there, Zach Allen."

"And hello to you, Lia Langston. Fancy meeting you here."

"And you as well." She nodded.

He held out his hand. "Care to take an evening stroll with me? No jokes. I promise."

He sounded so formal for someone his age, and Lia sort of liked it. A gentleman in beach bum clothing? She hesitated only slightly, then took his hand. "Sure. I'd like that."

ZACH TOOK ADVANTAGE OF THE situation and didn't drop Lia's hand. In fact, he held it along the way on their leisurely stroll toward the pier. The younger crowd was naturally drawn toward the bonfire, which was why he wanted to go in the opposite direction.

"Have you been to the pier?"

Lia looked at him and smiled. "Yes. Many times. My girlfriends and I have been coming here for a few years. Spring break. Holiday weekends when we can. Usually a week in the summer."

Zach thought about that. "Yes, you mentioned that in passing this morning." They approached a large piece of driftwood, half submerged in the sand. He motioned with his free hand. "Want to sit?"

She looked at him and their gazes connected. "Sure." Her lips curled into a smile. He sat on the wood, tugged her closer, and she sat beside him.

"So, what about you? Tell me the Zach Allen story."

He stared off into the ocean. The lights of the pier house penetrated the growing darkness, so much so that he couldn't really see the house around the lights, which looked like small beacons set in the sky. "Ah, that story," he said. "It's rather boring."

"Probably not as boring as mine."

"Want to trade stories?"

Lia shrugged. "Okay. You, first. I already asked." She grinned again, and Zach's heart melted a little.

"That you did. Well, let's see. I live here most summers with my Aunt Grace. She owns the Inn, down the way. Have since I was a little kid, after my mom died. My home is in New Hampshire where my dad lives now. No siblings. I work for Grace in the busy season and generally help her out when I can. I majored in business and minored in IT at the University of New Hampshire, and I'll finish up my MBA online later this year. I've lived here at the Inn for the past year. There you have it."

Lia stared. "Impressive."

He chuckled. "Not so much."

"I'm sorry about your mom."

He nodded. "More about that another time. Now, you." He'd rather hear about her than talk about himself.

Taking a deep breath, Lia also stared off into the sea. "Typical Midwest upbringing," she started. "In Chicago. My dad works downtown, a stockbroker. My mom works from home, running a real estate staging business. She also does volunteer work. No siblings, either. Dad put me through school. I didn't have to work. Just graduated, as I told you earlier, from ECU—Eastern Carolina University. Dad wanted me to go to an Ivy League school somewhere, but I chose differently. It was the only thing I've ever bucked him on, but I fell in love with the campus. So different from Chicago. Besides, the mountains are close and the beach is just seven hours away."

"Not a bad drive. Closer than coming from New Hampshire, for sure."

"Yep. So, I'm working here for the summer—sort of my last hurrah, I suppose—before heading into Corporate America in the fall."

"You have a job yet?"

"Very close. I've interviewed, and it went well. Dad says he has an inside track, so we will see." She looked at him.

Zach thought about that and studied her face. "And you are okay with that?"

"What?"

"Your dad having an inside track."

She shrugged. "He says that's the way it's done."

"Ah." Zach pulled his gaze away.

"What does that mean?"

He looked at her. "I guess that's the difference between Chicago and New Hampshire." He paused and watched her eyes dark back and forth.

"What do you mean?"

He clasped her hand tighter, suddenly afraid that he'd stepped his foot in it and that she might pull away. He didn't want her to pull away. "Just that there is no way in hell I'd let my dad pull strings for me to get a job."

Her facial expression went blank. "There's nothing wrong with having connections."

Time for him to change the subject. "No, of course not." He gripped her hand tighter. "You know, I'm surprised I've not seen you around before now. The past couple of years, I mean."

"I suppose we didn't travel in the same circles."

"Probably not."

"We, my girlfriends and I, kept to the house a lot and the beach. Occasionally, a restaurant or shopping. That's about it." She looked off for a moment, then back. "Zach, thank you again for helping me this morning."

Grinning, he turned slightly her way. "I was happy to help the damsel in distress."

She snorted. "Oh, please."

"Seriously, I didn't mind. I was happy to help you."

"Oh, so you have a savior complex?"

"Ah, no. I just like to consider myself a good guy and a gentleman. You can thank my Aunt Grace for that."

"She sounds like a very important person in your life."

He nodded. "She is. Perhaps you'll meet her one day."

Lia smiled. "I would like that."

A bit of awkwardness snaked between them, and they both fell silent, looking at the ocean. Zach realized that his hand holding hers had suddenly turned sweaty.

"Ready to head back?" He stood and dropped her hand.

"Sure."

They walked for a while, occasionally brushing elbows or backs of hands. As they stopped in front Tequila Sunrise, Zach turned toward her. "Lia, I'd like to see you again. Tomorrow? Are you free?"

She hesitated. "I think so. The girls and I are not big on making plans."

"Have you seen Sea Glass Inn? I'll show you around."

"And I can meet Aunt Grace?"

"Of course."

"I'd love to, Zach. That would be nice."

For a moment, their gazes danced and just when Zach was prepared to lean in—his plan was to give her a quick peck on the cheek—voices shouted from the dune walk and deck above, and Lia stepped back.

"Lia!"

"What in the world?" Lia jerked her head toward the noise. *Was Zach just about to kiss me?*

Her friends—the four of them minus Willow—came running down from the deck and over the dune walk. In pairs, first Alice and Maggie and followed by Wren and Julia, they scrambled down the steps and rushed forward, tripping through the sand while wearing flip flops.

Maggie finally tossed hers off and stopped abruptly before Lia and Zach, out of breath. "Lia! We didn't know where you'd gone."

Alice joined Maggie, also winded. "You and Willow slipped away, and then nothing."

"You left your cell phone behind," Maggie added. "We thought you'd been kidnapped!"

"Kidnapped? Oh, good gracious. I just went for a walk." Lia caught Zach's eye. He seemed a bit amused, if the grin on his face meant anything.

Julia broke in. "But you didn't tell us. You always tell us."

"Well, I guess I didn't this time. I'm fine, you all. So, cool it." Lia ran her gaze over the group, who stood there like they were expecting her to say more. "What?"

"You always take your cell phone." Maggie fiddled with her flip flops.

"So, we called Willow," Wren interrupted, "because we know hers is always attached to her body somewhere."

"And what did she tell you?" Lia arched a brow, studying Wren.

"She said she lost track of you after she

went to the bonfire with her drug dealer and...."

Lia looked to Zach, who still appeared amused by the entire scenario, and possibly alarmed at the cacophony of words and phrases darting out from her friends. The women chattered on in the background, but Lia was momentarily caught spellbound by the mesmerizing look on Zach's face. He was actually enjoying the onslaught from her girlfriends.

"I'm sorry." She mouthed the words.

He shrugged, his grin broadening across his face.

She turned back to the women. "I'm fine. Now stop prattling about like little old ladies." She took a step closer to Zach. "Have you met Zach Allen?"

"The tire change guy?" Maggie took a half step forward.

Lia rolled her eyes. "Yes."

The twittering stopped. All four women's mouths clamped closed, and their heads turned toward Zach. "No, we haven't," Alice said.

"All right." Lia waved a hand in Zach's direction. "Ladies, this is Zach, the "tire guy" from this morning. And Zach? These are my friends Alice, Maggie, Wren, and Julia." She pointed to each as she introduced them. "My best friends. Oh, and Willow, Wren's twin sister, is down at the bonfire, I imagine."

"With her drug dealer." Zach affirmed.

Lia rolled her eyes. "Oh, good God, no. I'll tell you about that tomorrow."

"Tomorrow?" Maggie raised an eyebrow. "You're going to see him tomorrow, Lia?"

And the next day and the next day, if he'll let me. Lia looked at Zach, dismissed the women, and smiled. "Yes, I believe so. Meet you here at... What time?"

"Can I give you a ring? I need to check my work schedule."

"Oh, sure."

Maggie blurted out, "Her number is 773-209-7...."

Lia shot Maggie a look. "Stop. I believe I can handle the details, Maggie."

"And thus, our clue to leave," said Alice, turning back to the steps. "Come on, girls. Let's go. We have drinks getting warm on the deck."

Lia watched them step away and exhaled. "Whew. They can sometimes be intense."

Zach laughed out loud. Turning, she gave him her full attention. His amused expression suddenly turned a bit more serious. Leaning in, he placed a forefinger under her chin, tipping her head up slightly. As his lips met hers in a sweet, soft, lingering kiss, Lia closed her eyes and let the sensation wash over her as he brushed his lips across hers.

Her eyes closed, and she savored the kiss for several seconds before opening them again.

"I can't wait to see you again tomorrow," he whispered, his head still slanting toward hers.

She dipped her head in a slight nod, keeping eye contact. "Same."

"Call the Inn in the morning and ask for me. If I'm not available, leave your number and I'll call you back."

"That sounds like a plan."

His gaze dropped to her lips. "Um-hmm." Again, his mouth skimmed hers, and his soft kiss played over her lips. Lia rested her hands on each of Zach's biceps.

He took a step back, breaking the kiss, distancing himself. "I better go before I get carried away."

Lia giggled. She felt practically giddy inside. "I'll see you tomorrow, Zach."

"Yes." He took a few steps toward the direction of the bonfire. "Sweet dreams, Lia."

"You too," she echoed back. Lia was fairly certain that her dreams tonight would indeed be sweet. "Good night."

LIA AND ZACH WORKED OUT THE arrangements to meet the following morning, and she got away from Tequila Sunrise without prying eyes and probing questions. In fact, when Zach picked her up a little before eleven o'clock that morning, Alice was the only other person up, nursing a cup of coffee in a deck chair, and oblivious as Lia scribbled a note and left it on the kitchen breakfast bar then slipped out the front door of the house.

Zach waited for her in the Sea Glass Inn truck. Her heart fluttered as she tripped down the flight of stairs off the porch and anticipated spending a little time with him today. As she entered the passenger side of the truck and slammed the door closed, she looked at Zach. "Whew. I escaped. Let's get the heck out of here!"

His broad smile captivated, and Lia's heart felt full and happy as they locked gazes.

"Your wish is my command, Miss. To the Inn?"

"Absolutely. I can't wait to see it."

He grinned and shifted into reverse, backed the truck up, then headed out of the short drive. After they got on the highway, he glanced her way. "I mentioned to Aunt Grace that you were coming and, of course, she decided that lunch was in order."

"Oh, she doesn't have to do that." Lia didn't want her to go to any trouble.

"Are you kidding? She's a southern woman, and when friends visit, you feed them. I think we will have time for a quick tour of the grounds first, then back to her place for lunch."

"But I'm sure she's busy. Seriously. We could grab lunch elsewhere."

He stopped for a traffic light and tossed her a very serious look. "Are you trying to get me into trouble? If I don't deliver you for lunch, I won't hear the end for years, and I'm likely to be punished and sent to my bed without my supper."

Lia studied him, pondering that. "Wow. She is a tough cookie."

"That she is."

"I'm looking forward to lunch, then."

Zach shifted and sped up. "Good. She's looking forward to it, too." He gave her a wink and returned to his driving. "As am I."

That wink sent Lia's heart spiraling, and she had a difficult time keeping her eyes off him for the fifteen minutes drive to the inn. Which was even more incredible—the Inn, that is—when they pulled into the parking lot, and she saw it in person. It was more beautiful than she had previously imagined.

Three white buildings loomed before them —all on stilts, windows framed with black shutters and lined up facing the ocean like soldiers braced for the oncoming. She supposed they were braced for the wind and waves—and perhaps family vacationers. The morning sun sparkled off the white walls, reflecting an aura

Lia could only describe in her head as *magical beachism*.

She chuckled to herself. Had she just invented a new phraseology about the beach? Magical beachism seemed perfectly logical to her.

They exited the truck. "All these buildings are part of the Inn?" Lia noticed a sign in the front of the middle building. Written in a large scroll were the words: *Sea Glass Inn at Tuckaway Bay*. And then beneath those words: *Welcome to your escape.* All the words were painted in crisp turquoise and set against a freshly painted white background.

Closing her eyes, she could hear the ocean, and Lia sighed. "Oh yes. Magical beachism."

Zach chuckled. "What?"

She blinked and looked at him. "This place is like magical beachism."

Grinning, he took her arm. "You're hired to lead the marketing team. C'mon, let's go see more." He led her down a walkway between two buildings, which turned out to be a beach access. Within a few steps, they wove through the dunes and stepped out onto the beach.

"This is one of three beach accesses on the property," he told her. "The beach is private to the Inn. The public beach access is to the north, and to the south, there is one at the pier. And then behind us to the right...."

Lia turned and followed the direction of

where he looked.

"...is the pool and gazebo area."

Which was mighty impressive. The pool sat in front of the main building. On this, the ocean side of the buildings, all the rooms were lined with balconies. "Does each room have a balcony?"

"Yes. The suites are on this side, and there is a balcony off the bedroom and also one off the living room area. Every suite has an ocean view. The rooms at the backside are single rooms without a view but offer the same beach private beach experience at a lower price. Some families like that."

"That is awesome."

"Yes."

Her gaze traveled over the area and settled on the far corner. "Is that a tiki bar over there at the end?"

He nodded. "It's open after June fifteenth, when tourist season officially starts."

Lia squinted. "And what's beyond the tiki bar? I see some dunes and sea oats and more buildings."

Zach glanced her way. "You're very observant. Those are the cottages. There are six of them. One is out of commission for this summer for renovations, and one of them has a full-time resident. They are more private than the suites offered in the main buildings."

"I'd love to see them too, if we have time."

Zach sidled up next to her. "Sure."

With Zach so close, Lia felt her breath slipping out of her lungs, and she almost felt dizzy. He was tall. Taller than she'd remembered, either that or she was standing in a hole in the sand! Or maybe it was the sun, which radiated behind him, sparking off his hair and giving off a halo effect around his head. Lia blinked and glanced away.

"Wow, that sun is bright."

Zach took her hand. "It is. Let's head over to the cottages."

They had only taken a few steps when a woman's voice called out from above. "Hey you two! It's almost time for lunch. Head up this way soon!"

Lia shielded her eyes with her hand and looked up to see a woman standing on a balcony on the top floor of the three-story building, waving and looking down at them. "Is that Aunt Grace?"

"In the flesh," Zach replied. Then, waving back at his aunt, he said, "We will be right up."

Grace faded into the shadow of the balcony.

Zach grasped Lia's hand.

"Let's see the cottages after lunch. Time to meet the boss."

Lia didn't know why her stomach felt on edge, but it was. Zack held her hand through the access and back to the middle building.

They took an old elevator up to the third floor and he rapped on the door of a room about halfway down the narrow hallway—she assumed the hallway between the suites on the left, and regular hotel rooms on the right. The whole thing felt ridiculously like she was meeting her boyfriend's parents for the first time.

She'd done that a time or two, and this definitely felt like those times.

"Relax," Zach said. "She's going to love you."

Why that mattered, she didn't know. Suddenly, it felt like her life was in some sort of whirlwind, and she wondered if, when the wind stopped twirling, would she be the same person?

The door burst open. Framed there was a woman Lia guessed to be in her mid-sixties, short gray hair, slightly overweight, and attractive. Her blue eyes twinkled, and her drawn-on brows arched at the sight of her.

"Well, well. At long last. Welcome, Lia."

Lia glanced at Zach, who put his hand on her back. "After you," he said.

She looked again at the woman. "It's wonderful to meet you, Mrs. Allen."

"Grace," she offered. "Or Aunt Grace, if you like." She gasped her hand. "Now, come on in and let's get a look at you. It's about damn time my nephew brought home a woman."

Three

If she thought her first impression of the inn and Aunt Grace a whirlwind, Lia had no clue what was to come with the ensuing lunch conversation. Grace definitely seized the dialogue and had specific questions for Lia. From time to time, as she caught Zach's eye, Lia realized he was possibly a tad bit embarrassed at the line of questioning.

Aunt Grace drove the conversation toward her family, her college studies, her career aspirations. What did she think of marriage, did she want children and how many, and what was she looking for in a life partner?

That last part was embarrassing, and Lia hemmed and hawed long enough in responding, that Zach hijacked the conversation and turned to a different subject.

Thankfully.

"Aunt Grace, Lia came up with a phrase

this morning that might be worked into a new marketing campaign for the Inn," he said.

"Really?" Grace's eyes widened. "Tell me more."

"You tell her, Lia."

Lia's head jerked, and she looked at Zach. "Oh no, you can."

He stared, then focused on his aunt. "She called the area *magical beachism*."

Aunt Grace looked her way. "Do you know anything about marketing, dear?" Her stare penetrated, and Lia gulped a little.

"I had one class. Definitely not an expert."

"But you could learn."

"Oh, I suppose so but—"

"Well, that's good enough for me." Grace looked at Zach. "I think she's perfect and of course, she should stay here at the Inn."

Lia's head spun. She glanced from Grace to Zach and back to Grace again. "What? I don't understand."

Zach frowned. "Aunt Grace, what are you talking about?"

"The manager's job, of course."

He shook his head. "No. I didn't bring Lia here about the manager's job. I brought her here because I wanted you to meet her. She's a friend, and she's here all summer, so I thought we'd get to know her better. She's not a job candidate."

Grace stood. "Oh pooh. I know that, Zachary.

"Wait." Lia's anxiety escalated. "I already have a job, and I start Monday. I am not looking for a job."

"That's right, Grace. Lia has a job at the Seaside Shoppes."

Grace eyed Lia. "That will never do. You're much too valuable to be working retail all day. I need you here."

"But I can't...."

"Nonsense. You'll stay here, too. Zach, set her up in the Pelican's Nest."

"What? Oh no, I couldn't," Lia protested.

"Aunt Grace?" Zach stood and approached his aunt. "The Pelican's Nest? You want her to stay there?"

Grace eyed her nephew. "Yes. Pelican's Nest. It's out of commission for the summer, right? We already decided that and weren't counting on the income. We can work on the renovations during the day while Lia is at work. That is, if she doesn't mind living in the space while we are doing upgrades. It's just paint and carpet and a kitchen upgrade, the counters and flooring. Lia?"

"Pelican's Nest?"

"It's one of the cottages, Lia."

"Oh." Her gaze darted about. "Aunt Grace, that is very generous of you, but I couldn't. I have an apartment lined up already—I'm sharing with two other women who also work at the Shoppes. That was part of the deal for the job. While I greatly appreciate this opportunity, I couldn't possibly." To say she was a tad overwhelmed at this turn of events, was an understatement.

Grace frowned. "You mean you're getting a deal on your rent because you are summer help at the Seaside Shoppes? So that's how Marilyn is working it now. Hmmm..." She thought about that for a minute.

Lia wondered just exactly what kind of predicament she'd just landed herself in.

Grace drummed her fingers on a side table, glanced off to stare into the ocean for a moment, then back to Lia. "Did you sign a lease?"

"No, not really. Just an agreement."

"The housing comes with the job, you say? But what if you don't take the job, then that gets you out of the housing agreement. Correct?"

"I suppose so, but I need the job. I can't stay here all summer without a job. That was the deal I made with my father."

"Oh, you'll have a job." Grace stood and looked at Zach. "Tell Miranda to talk to Sarah and get the Pelican cleaned up by Monday. And tell Joshua to get the manager's office back in order, cleaned and organized by Monday too." She turned to Lia then and studied her. "I can meet your salary from the mall and increase it by one-hundred dollars a week. Plus, housing is free. Is your father a businessman?"

"Yes. Stockbroker."

"Good. Then he'll understand the benefits of this arrangement. If he has issues, tell him to call me. You said your degree was in business, right?"

"Yes, with an emphasis on non-profit management, though..." Lia looked at Zach, then back to Grace. "I don't mind saying that I am totally confused here. Can someone please explain to me what is happening?"

Zach made eye contact, grinning. "Aunt Grace just hired you."

Lia felt her eyes widen. "Doing what? I don't know a thing about hotels. What would I be doing?"

Grace took a step her way and reached for her hand. "Whatever I tell you to do, Lia. You'll manage things, and you'll learn. Now, look. What are you going to gain skill-wise by working retail? I realize you get to live at the beach for the summer and make a little money. But here, you can really experience the business side of things, learning as you go, so to speak, and gain some skills that can move you forward in your next job."

"But I already have committed to the dress shop. And the apartment. I'm not sure I can get out of it."

Grace fluttered a hand. "Oh pooh. I'll talk

to Marilyn Devers. She owns the Shoppes, you know. We go way back to elementary school, and I don't mind telling you that stealing you away from her gives me quite a bit of pleasure. The twit stole my date for the homecoming dance back in '54."

Lia looked to Zach for help. "I..."

"Just go with it, Lia. The cards have been dealt."

"So, I'm working here?"

He grinned. "It's settled."

"But I didn't say yes."

Grace interrupted. "You didn't say no, either, and I'll take that as a yes. Now, let's finish lunch. Miranda made strawberry shortcake for dessert. After, I'll show you around some more. That work for the two of you?" The older woman bounced her gaze from Lia to Zach.

"Yes, ma'am," Zach said.

Lia followed suit. "Yes, of course." Then she added, for good measure. "But shouldn't I call Mrs. Devers myself and tell her I will need to decline the job offer?"

Aunt Grace gave her a stern look. "No indeedy. Nothing for you to do on your end. I'll handle it from here. You are on my clock starting Monday morning at eight. Enjoy the rest of this week. Now, let's dig into those strawberries. The market over on the mainland had a special on them yesterday. Plumpest berries I've ever seen."

Lia half-listened as Grace chattered on in the background. Her summer plans had just gone awry, lickety-split. Was she okay with that? She hadn't entirely processed things yet, of course, so would she regret this decision—that she really didn't make herself—later. Was she allowing herself to be a pushover? To get railroaded into something she didn't really want?

If she had any doubts, she should just back out now. Right? Before Grace called Mrs. Devers?

Zach's gaze caught hers then, and she warmed at his sexy half-grin. All the tension in her body suddenly released. She smiled back, and her gut suddenly grew a swarm of butterflies. In a rather shy gesture, Zach glanced at his strawberries, then slowly lifted his head to look back at her again. This time, he beamed, and her heart leaped in response.

It was all okay. Everything was going to be just fine.

THE GIRLS ALL LEFT ON SATURDAY. LIA watched Alice and Maggie, the last two of the group to leave—besides Lia, of course—pull out of the driveway in their respective vehicles mid-morning. They were headed back to their hometowns for summer jobs of their own, while they searched for future career positions. Maggie was from Rocky Mount, a few hours inland from the beach. Alice lived in Tuckaway Bay, so her drive home was short.

Julia left early that morning to head to Louisville, and was excited to see her boyfriend, Mark. He had popped the question a few weeks ago. In typical Julia fashion, she was putting him off—even though all the girls knew she would marry him, eventually. The pair had been together since high school. The drive would take her a couple of days, so Lia hoped she took the time to think.

Wren and Willow grew up in Long Beach, so they left in the wee hours for Norfolk to catch their flight back to California. Both women were footloose for the summer, and Lia hoped they figured out their next-steps plan, now that their father had passed. He'd left them with a healthy inheritance of cash and property to deal with. Lia worried about Willow more than Wren—she'd always been a loose cannon—but Lia also knew the sisters were protective of each other.

"Until next year, ladies." She whispered the words to herself. Of course, no one could hear her.

It had been an awesome week, but now the rest of their lives waited in the wings. The six of them were set for new adventures, and hers was waiting for her up the coast, over at the Inn.

At least for the summer.

She glanced back at Tequila Sunrise and tossed her bags into the trunk of her Honda roadster, ready for whatever the summer would bring. The picture tucked in her head was definitely different from the one she had formed there a few weeks earlier. The tickle of anticipation in her gut excited her more than she'd been in a long, long time.

ZACH WATCHED FOR LIA'S RED SPORTS car to make the turn off the bypass and travel down the side road toward the resort property. While he sat in the truck waiting, the driver's side door open so he could get some air, he thought about the how his aunt had turned the tables on both he and Lia a few days earlier.

He recalled their conversation after he took Lia back to her beach rental.

"What was all of that about, Aunt Grace?"

She shrugged. "Well, for one, you never bring women here, so I figured she was special."

"We just met. I am still trying to get to know her."

Her eyes twinkled. "And now you will. I'm sure you'll be seeing her often. Daily, likely."

Zach sighed. Was the old woman playing matchmaker? "So, you like her?"

"She's a beautiful young woman, Zach. Smart and articulate. She doesn't need to be stuck in a dress shop for the summer."

"But maybe that's what she wants?"

"I don't think she knows for sure what she wants. I am just giving a little nudge."

His brow arched. "And you know what she wants?"

"I have a pretty good idea."

"But how?"

Grace smiled. "Women's intuition."

"Ah." He wouldn't touch that with a ten-foot pole.

"It will all work out fine. You watch," she said.

Yeah. The wait and see approach. He'd heard that one before.

Glancing back to the road, he watched Lia's car turn into the parking lot and dismissed the memory of the conversation. He stood and waved her toward the truck. "Over here!"

She pulled up beside him. "Hi, Zach."

"Hey, Lia. Follow me. I'll take you to the cottages."

She gave him a brief salute, then backed up to let him out so she could follow.

A few minutes later, they drove through the separate, private entrance to the cottages. Zach parked his truck in one of the two spaces in front of the Pelican's Nest and Lia nestled her car in the space beside him.

"Well, here we are," she said, exiting the car. "I'll get my bags."

Zach met her at the trunk. "Here. I'll carry them."

He did, and she followed him toward the Pelican's Nest cottage. They traveled up the five steps to the porch, and Zach set the bags down beside him while he pushed a key into the lock, and then shoved the door inward. Turning to Lia, he watched as her gaze played over the porch and the building.

"This is really nice, Zach. I don't know what to say. The porch is so cute! All the beach chairs with pillows, and the hanging plants, and the wicker tables and all."

He nodded and glanced about. "Aunt Grace loves the southern charm. The inside is nice, too. But remember, starting in about a week, this place will turn chaotic as new carpet is laid, and the painting starts."

She turned to him. "It's okay. I'm happy to be right here. I can practically live on this porch! It will be fine. Oh, Zach?"

"Yes?"

"Where do you stay? I mean. Here at the Inn? Or elsewhere?"

Zach tried to stifle his grin, but couldn't. Suddenly, he was reminded of the matchmaking conversation he'd had with Aunt Grace a few days ago.

"I live here, in the Tortoise Shell Cottage."

"Oh? And where is that?" She glanced about.

Zach sucked in a breath. "Not far."

"Zach..."

He ticked his head toward the end of the porch. "Right next door, Lia. I'm the cottage over there."

She followed his gaze, and said, "Well now. That is interesting." Turning back and taking a step closer to him, Lia looked up into his face. "I'm not sure what I am getting myself into for this summer, Zach Allen," she said, then paused, searching his eyes. "But I'm sort of excited to see how it all plays out."

Grinning, she leaned in and placed a quick kiss on Zach's cheek.

But he wasn't about to let her get off that easily. "Oh, and why is that?" He fiddled with a strand of her hair and teasingly tugged.

She cocked her head to the side and grinned. "Because I've decided that I like you a little bit, Zach Allen."

"Oh? And when did you decide that, Lia Langston?"

"I think it was when you made me think you would not help me on the side of the road."

"Ah. I thought you were a little ticked at me at that point."

Her upturned, playful smile just about did him in. Pulling her closer, their bodies met. "I was, but then I remembered I like a guy with a sense of humor."

"You do, huh?"

"Umhmm." Zach dipped his head closer. "May I kiss you again, Lia Langston?"

"On one condition."

"And what is that?"

"Kiss me like you mean it."

Four

Late Summer, August

LIA CAREFULLY PICKED HER WAY OVER the large rocks leading to the side of the lighthouse facing the ocean, wanting only to get to the large rock and sit, alone with her thoughts. The beach was anything but quiet, but there on the rock, she was alone, and that's all she wanted right now. Even as dusk fell, she wondered if she'd made the right decision. She wanted to think, and she wasn't sure much thinking would happen here, with late summer crowds getting a little rowdy down the beach. Only a couple more weeks of summer fun remained.

She and Zach came here often when they wanted to be alone and away from the Inn. He was working late this evening, however, helping Grace decide about fall plantings and winter maintenance on the buildings, pool, and cottages.

Those discussions were unlike some she and Grace already had, but the older woman relied on Zach's expertise as far as which buildings and cottages needed upgrades and repair work, and which didn't for this go-round. Those things Lia didn't know for certain, of course. She could only advise on the popularity of the rooms, and which were likely to sell out in the fall and spring, according to what was going on locally to draw tourists into the areas during the off season.

It had been a busy day, and an even busier summer. While she and Zach were inseparable most of the time, the season flew by all too quickly, as summers often do.

In early September, the tourist season would be over. Tuckaway Bay would slow down the week after Labor Day, and the Inn would operate on diminished capacity from there until May next year. In two weeks, Grace wouldn't need a summer manager for the hotel, and Lia would head back to Chicago.

But just as well, she supposed. The job offer her Dad had navigated for her over the summer came though, and she was expected to begin her position as a grant writer for The

Food Exchange, an up-and-coming non-profit in the city focused on food scarcity, started the first week of September. It was an excellent opportunity to get her foot in the door of the non-profit world and to explore her possibilities for the future.

Her heart ached just thinking about it, though. She hadn't told Zach yet.

"Hey! There you are. I've been looking for you."

Speak of the devil.

Seeing Zach made Lia's heart lighter, and she instantly felt better. "Hi! What are you doing here? I thought you and Grace had decisions to make."

"We do. We did. All done." He sat beside her, scooted closer, and wrapped an arm around her shoulders. "Besides, I was missing you. May I join you?"

She grinned and peered into his eyes. "Always. You know that."

He nodded. "That I do."

His kiss lit up her insides the instant his mouth touched hers. Lia felt alive and sparkly when she was around Zach. She wondered if she glowed as his lips brushed across hers, teased and tasted. No one ever made her feel as special, or as wanted, as Zach. No one had ever kissed her like Zach kissed her.

She broke away, sighed, and pulled back to

look into his eyes. Her palms cupped his cheeks and she whispered, "I do love you, Zach Allen."

"And I love you back, Lia Langston."

He kissed her again, long and lazy, while the crowd about twenty feet or so away from the lighthouse grew noisier. When Zach pulled back this time, he asked her about dinner. "Have you eaten? I'm starved. I thought maybe we could have a late dinner at the Pier House. I'm craving crab and wine and perhaps a late night snuggle after."

The thought of all of that—every single bit of it—made Lia happy. Why couldn't life just stay like this forever? "I think that is an exceptionally good idea."

"Well, let's go." Zach stood and held out his hand.

Lia took it, and he hoisted her to her feet, wrapping his arms around her. For a lingering moment, he stared into her eyes once more, almost to where Lia didn't know whether to kiss him again or turn away.

Then he spoke. "I love you more than my life, Lia. I hope you know that."

Her heart danced. "I do, Zach. And I love you right back, just the same."

"Good." He quickly placed another kiss on her lips. "Let's go get that crab."

The dinner turned out to be just as wonderful as their few moments spent behind the lighthouse. Zach had reserved a table overlooking the ocean, surprising Lia. It was all there, like he had said—the wine, the crab, and a fabulous chocolate dessert—and Lia felt incredibly full by the time they finished their meal.

She tucked her arm into Zach's as they left the pier. "I'm glad we walked. I need to work off that meal. It was lovely, Zach. Thank you."

"My pleasure." He squeezed her hand tucked into his elbow. "I enjoyed both the food and the company." He leaned in for a quick kiss. "Especially the company."

She silently agreed, smiling. They strolled the beach toward the Inn, their path lit by the lights of houses along the way, and a full moon trailing them over the ocean. As they approached the back entrance to the cottages, Zach turned to her. "Lia?"

"Hm?"

"I want you to stay."

Lia stumbled, and he caught her up, holding her close. Looking into his eyes, she sensed the sincerity of his words.

"What do you mean, Zach?"

He pushed out a breath, glanced off for a few seconds, then turned back to look at her. "I can't bear to think of you leaving. What are your plans? Did you hear about Chicago yet?"

She had to be honest with him. As much as

she dreaded telling him, she had to do it. "Yes. I heard from them earlier in the week."

"And you didn't tell me?"

"I was waiting for the right time, Zach."

He raked a hand over his head. "Well?"

"I got the job. I start in a couple of weeks."

Again, he blew out a breath and clutched his t-shirt at his chest. "Lia. What are you going to do? Are you going? Shouldn't we discuss this together?"

He was right. They should discuss it together. "Yes, of course. Because I need to know what you are doing, too. What about when you finish your MBA in December? What are your plans, then?"

He stepped back, shoving his hands into his jeans pockets. "Me? This isn't about me, Lia. It's about if you are leaving, or not."

"Zach, it is about us. We both have, or had, plans. We have degrees we've achieved and need to put to good use. We both need to consider our next steps carefully. I just haven't had time to think about it or process it all yet."

"You think I have?"

She shook her head. "No, I don't. I... Zach, part of the reason I hadn't told you is because I don't know what to do. I keep weighing the pros and cons. I want to make the right decision. For us. For me."

He drew her closer, his hands on her elbows. "Then let's escalate that a bit. Lia. I didn't exactly plan it like this, but I don't want to wait." He got down on one knee, settled himself there in the sand, and looked up at her. "I don't even have a ring yet, but I don't think you'll hold that against me." He took her left hand in his. "Lia Langston, I love you with all of my heart. I want to spend the rest of my life with you. I want to stay here, with you, in Tuckaway Bay forever. Will you marry me?"

Lia looked down into Zach's expectant face, knowing he wanted an answer. His words —all of them—were a mouthful and filled with so many insinuations for their futures she didn't even know where to start.

Except for one thing—she knew she couldn't give him the answer he wanted to hear.

"Oh, Zach..." She grasped his hand and tugged him to his feet. Pushing closer, she peered up into his eyes, cupping his face in her hands again, just like she did earlier at the lighthouse. "Zach. I love you. And someday, I want you to ask me that question again, and I want to say yes. Someday, I want to marry you. But right now, I'm simply going to say that I love you. I can't say yes. Not yet. I hope that will be enough."

His heart shattered. Zach wasn't sure that it was.

THE NEXT MORNING, HE PUSHED through the door of Lia's office and stood across the small room looking at her until she lifted her head and caught his eye. As their gazes mingled, anguish and remorse slammed into his chest. He yearned to rush to her and hold her.

He knew he had to hold back.

He had to make this right. Had to. And if that meant backing off from what he genuinely wanted for a while, he would do it. If he could.

"Zach..." Lia murmured. "Good morning. Had breakfast? Miranda made omelets, and I believe some are still out on the buffet in the dining room."

Taking strides across the floor and to her desk, Zach sat beside her. "Thanks. I had coffee back at the cottage. Lia, can we talk about last night?" His gut hurt, and his head had been busy with wayward thoughts all night. He'd barely slept. "Please?"

Laying a pen aside, she rotated in her chair and gave him her full attention. "Yes. I want to talk about it too."

He nodded. "Good. Okay."

"I do love you, Zach."

"I know that." He cleared his throat, looked down, and fiddled with his ball cap in his hands. "I jumped the gun last night. I'm sorry. It wasn't very romantic, and it wasn't the right time."

She touched his cheek. "I was romantic, Zach. The dinner, the beach, the moonlight... But yes, perhaps not the right time."

"I can wait, Lia." He'd wait forever if he had to. "For your answer."

He watched her gaze lower, playing over the desk, as if she were thinking about something. Perhaps trying to decide what to say. Her pause was killing him.

"Zach?"

"Yes?"

"I need to go back to Chicago. At least for a while. I need to see if I can do this work. If I like it. It's what I've been working toward for so long."

"I can understand that."

"So you are okay with it?"

He shook his head. "No. I'd be lying if I said I was."

"Why?"

"Because you won't come back. You think you will, but you won't. You'll get caught up in the work, the lifestyle, and before long, Tuckaway Bay, and I, will be just another summer memory."

"No. No, it won't, Zach."

"Oh, yes. That's the way it works, Lia."

"I will come back."

He stood. "Summer help never comes back. That's the law of averages."

Her puzzled look took him off guard. "What do you mean by that, Zach?"

"Summer help. You come, you break hearts, you leave."

She stood, too. "Is that all you think I am? Summer help?"

Shrugging, he said, "I don't know. Are you?"

"No! I thought I was much more than that to you."

"Of course you are." He paced away from the desk, then looked back. "That just seems the way things happen around here, though."

Lia pushed away from the desk and stepped closer to him. "Zach. Let's do this for a year. I'll go work in Chicago. You'll finish your MBA. We will do the long-distance thing for a few months and then in the spring, we can make some decisions."

He shook his head. "I don't know. I'm not sure we can make it work. I can't envision a long-distance relationship."

"Then you're not really willing to work on this then. Are you?" Lia's gaze played over his face for a moment, then she slowly turned and walked back to the desk, opened her laptop, and fiddled with the mouse. There were tears in her eyes and knowing her, she was trying hard not to let them fall.

"I have a lot of work to do this morning, Zach. I need to push pause on this conversation."

"Because of the work? It can wait," he told her.

"No, because I need to sort things out in my head and in my heart. Please, I need some time."

A knock sounded at the door and Zach looked that way as his Aunt Grace bustled in.

"Hey there, you two," she said, looking directly at him. "Zach, the toilet in 315 is on the blink. Can you give it a look, please?"

That was the last thing he wanted to do at this moment, but it was his job. "Sure. I'll get right on it."

"Good." She shooed him toward the door. "I have something go over with Lia, anyway. Urgent business. Let me know if that thing can be fixed. If not, buy another one and get a plumber in there."

"All right, Aunt Grace. I got it." He glanced at Lia, searching her misty eyes. "See you later?"

She nodded. "Of course."

ZACH LEFT. LIA'S HEART PLUMMETED TO her gut. And she watched as Grace Allen ambled across the room toward her. To say she wasn't in the mood for Grace right now was an understatement. What tasks had she invented for her this time?

"You've done a great job this summer, Lia. I couldn't be more pleased."

That surprised Lia a little and was not what she expected. "Well, thank you. I appreciate that." She closed the laptop lid and settled back into her chair. "What's can I do for you this morning?"

Grace stopped beside the desk and smiled. "I had a feeling about you right from the beginning and I was right. You've turned out to be a top-notch manager."

Again, Lia was taken aback. Where was the line of dialogue heading? "I guess that minor in non-profit management came in handy for something," Lia said. "Even if this is a for-profit establishment."

"You have a good head on your shoulders. No doubt the degree helped, but you've got a lot of common sense, and you make damn good business decisions."

"I'm glad you think so."

"I do. Look. I'll cut to the chase, Lia. I want to offer you a full-time position here at the Inn. In fact, I'm considering acquiring more properties and I'll need someone to manage the whole kit-and-kaboodle. You're a whiz with marketing and understanding the customer base. You've increased our efficiency

THAT ONE SUMMER

and can manage staff very well. I think you have the right skills. What do you say?"

Stunned at the offer, Lia stared at her. "Oh, Aunt Grace. I don't know. What a fabulous offer, but... This is really a surprise and...."

"And what?"

"Well, I already have a job waiting for me back home. I start in two weeks."

Grace waved her hand. "Nonsense. What skills can you learn there than you can't learn here?"

She'd heard this speech before, at the beginning of the summer. Back then, she'd been bamboozled away from the dress shop job to work here at the Inn. Before she knew it, her plans had changed, and her summer was on a different course.

But that had turned out well, hadn't it?

Except, she'd fallen in love with Zach, and now she'd broken his heart—as well as her own.

Should she let Grace Allen commandeer the rest of her life, like she had her summer? When was she going to step up and speak for herself, define her future on her own terms?

Lia cleared her throat and sat up a little straighter in the chair. "Like I said, Aunt Grace, it's a very generous offer and I am very appreciative. I'm quite flattered, actually, but I need to discuss this with my family, and—"

"Lia, you're a college graduate. A grown woman. Not a child."

"I know, but...."

"Think about it. Will you? I insist. I'm not likely to take no for an answer."

To say she was a little stunned at Aunt Grace's response was an understatement. Was she trying to force her hand?

"It's all too much. I don't know where to turn, what to think."

The waves licked at the rocks below them at the lighthouse. The tide was rising, the moon waning in the distance. But Zach and Lia had sat there for over an hour, trying to talk. To sift through the mess of their summer's end.

"It doesn't have to be this difficult, Lia. Really, it doesn't."

She shook her head. "How so? This is eating me up inside. You, too."

"I know." He shifted and took her hand. "I can make it easy for us both. Just marry me. Problem solved." Zach searched her eyes. He wished he could dive deeper inside of those orbs to fully appreciate what was going on with her. Suddenly, he was not above begging. "Stay with me. You can run the Inn. I'll finish my MBA and help with the maintenance. I can increase the IT capacity over time and eventually, we can make the Inn our family business. We can build a happy life here, Lia. I know it."

The look she gave him then was full of confusion. "Zach, I love you. But marriage... Not yet. It's just not that easy. You know I'm expected back in Chicago. Dad put himself on the line with his clients and..." She didn't finish. They'd been over this a hundred times.

"Lia. If you leave, I'll never see you again."

"That's not true! Stop saying that. I'll come back. I love you!"

"I love you, too. And I need you in my life, Lia. I need you here with me."

She pulled back, a puzzled expression on her face. "Zach, don't pressure me. Don't make me choose between my father's wishes and you."

"Whose life are you going to live, Lia? Yours or your father's?"

"Mine!"

"Really? Then stay. Your father will understand."

"No, he won't. He has pulled a lot of strings...."

Zach looked off across the horizon. His gut hurt and his head spun with the impossibilities of this repeated conversation. She would not budge. And he was unsure if he could continue it. He refused to think about her leaving. He'd just as soon rip out his heart. "The tide is coming in. We need to go." He stood and reached out for her. "Let's talk about this tomorrow."

Lia grasped his arm. "Wait, Zach. You understand, don't you?"

He made direct eye contact with her. *Understand? Understand what? That you are leaving me and never coming back?* "No, I don't. If you loved me, you would know what to do. You'd stay."

"Don't say that." She pushed up closer to him, her voice lowered. "I *do* love you."

"Then choose me, Lia. Choose us. Choose our life together here."

"Zach, please. I need to go back. Just for a year. Six months, maybe. Until you finish your MBA. Then I'll know. They we—"

"Then we'll be over."

She didn't miss a beat. "Then maybe we should just end it now."

Her words stabbed him to his very core. And he could tell they hurt her too. The look of horror on her face after having said them likely only mirrored the terror he felt inside his chest. He wanted to grab her and kiss her silly. To get the idea that they could be over out of her head. But he couldn't move. Shock, he guessed. All he could do was stare at her, like he was a stupid statue or something.

"Lia..." Her name fell from his lips on a hushed breath.

She stumbled past him on the rocks, tears in her eyes. A sob wrenched from her throat. Dumbfounded, he just stood there and watched her trip away...over the rocks, across the sand, and into the night.

He'd lost her. The love of his life. He'd lost her.

Twenty Years Later

"We'll need more ice by noon at this rate."

Lia Langston shoved a too-big bag of ice back into the freezer, praying it would stay put and not pop the freezer door open again. This was the only thing she disliked about Tequila Sunrise. There was never enough space for ice in the rickety old freezer-top refrigerator. Otherwise, the beachfront property was perfect. They had private beach access, the deck overlooked the ocean, and they were mere blocks from downtown Tuckaway Bay, where there were ample restaurants and bars.

Plus, history warranted that when she and her girlfriends were at the beach, ice was important.

"Anyone going into town today? Let's pick up a cooler."

Lia glanced toward her friends gathered around the kitchen island. The ocean was their backdrop, with sparkling waves glinting like diamonds in the bright morning sun. The full-length windows gave them a stunning view of the beach. The women were all dressed in beach attire. Suits and wraps were the mainstay wardrobe of the week—and while they may be covering a bit more flesh than they did twenty years ago, their wraps longer and their suits more substantial than the ones they wore in college, none of them truly gave a damn.

Lia smiled at the flit of memories racing through her head. Twenty-some years of coming to this beach—years of shared history between them. This was their twentieth annual summer's end trip since they graduated from college. The same week, the same beach house, the same beach town, every year.

There was no other beach for them than Tuckaway Bay Beach.

Lia had not missed a summer. It was the one thing she scheduled and didn't cancel, annually. Mostly, the other women were the same, with a few exceptions.

Five of them had arrived so far—Lia, Alice, Maggie, Wren, and Willow. They were waiting for Julia.

Alice still lived in Tuckaway Bay, living with her family in the house she grew up in, and was in charge of securing the annual rental. She was the reason they came to Tuckaway Bay, initially. The first time was a spring-break getaway from college when the girls were freshmen. Alice had talked so much about how she loved growing up in Tuckaway Bay, that by the time spring break rolled around, they were salivating to get out of the classroom and experience some serious sand and sangria. From then on, the girls got away from school whenever they could—long weekends, holidays, spring breaks—and then after graduation, they all marked their calendars with permanent ink for the last week in August. In perpetuity.

Alice opened the house yesterday, preparing for everyone to arrive. Maggie came with her, a last-minute change of plans. Lia arrived mid-morning, having driven down from Norfolk after her flight from Chicago the night before. The twins, Wren and Willow, showed up a few hours later, flying in on a red-eye from the west coast to Raleigh-Durham, then driving and crossing over at Roanoke Island.

Pouring a few glugs of tequila over the rocks in her glass, Lia added a wedge of lime. She anticipated that first crisp burn of alcohol on the back of her tongue. In Chicago, she was a wine girl. Here, it was tequila all day, all the way. It wasn't even noon, and yet they had already started cocktails. Glancing up, she caught Alice's eye. "Did you bring a cooler? Someone usually does."

To her left, Maggie piped up. "I usually do, but I didn't have time to get as organized as I would have liked this year. So much going on with the kids and getting Max ready to play dad for a week." She rambled on, glancing once at Alice, her voice trailing off. "Sorry about that. I can go get one." She pushed away from the island.

Lia slapped a hand on the bar in front of Maggie, who jumped like something had stung her. "Maggie! You sit tight. Not a big deal. It's happy time."

Lia grinned, trying to keep things light-hearted, but Maggie slowly deflated back down onto the bar stool and averted her gaze. She fiddled with her hair as she glanced again at Alice—who tilted her head a bit and blinked some sort of secret message.

"No worries, Mags," Lia added. "We'll round up a cooler later." Something was off, but she didn't know what. Maggie was generally bold and confident—but her subtle reaction to Lia's cooler question was different, somehow. Looking at Alice, she tried to catch her eye, hoping to get a clue of something, but Alice turned away.

Willow piped up. "Exactly. Let's fuel up. I'm taking my red cup for a walk on the beach before it gets too hot. I plan to be stoned or silly drunk within the hour. Anyone joining me?"

"Oh, my God, Willow. Did you bring weed?"

Willow tossed her a saucy grin.

Lia rolled her eyes. Willow, CEO of her own company, was ever still the rebel.

"Oh, please, Lia. Don't be a killjoy. We all smoked a joint once in a while back in the day. Besides, I've had a shit-hell week. I need this."

Wren hooked an arm into her sister's. "Seriously, Lia. We've had a freaking chaotic forty-eight hours."

Lia shrugged. "Hey, I get it. If this morning is any sign of what the rest of my week will be like, I might join you."

"Just don't smoke in the house," Alice interrupted, pushing past them all. "The owner will have a hissy if the place smells like pot when we check out."

"Yes, ma'am." Wren saluted and flashed her a silly grin.

They all scrambled, topping off their red cups with splashes of alcohol and scooting into flip-flops. The group scurried toward the door facing the ocean and spilled out onto the deck. Just as Lia and Alice were about to exit, a clackety-clack and a slow whistle sounded from the kitchen area. They turned and watched as the freezer door popped open and the bag of ice came tumbling out. Cubes skidded across the old plank wood floor like hockey pucks.

"Dammit." Alice stared at Lia. "Are you thinking what I am thinking?"

Lia nodded. "If you're thinking the freezer just died, then yes."

"Well hell's bells." Alice turned and waved to the girls. "You all go on. Minor emergency here. The fridge just bit the dust."

Groans came from the walkway over the dunes.

Alice turned back. "I'll call the landlord. Hopefully, we can get this fixed. In the meantime, do you mind running out for a cooler?"

"I don't mind at all." Lia looked down at herself, wondering if she should change. "Let me throw on some shorts first." She headed toward the stairs—the bedrooms were on the upper level.

Alice nodded, scrolling through her phone and mumbling. "Just looking for the number. There it is. Grace Allen."

Lia stopped in her tracks and blinked. A surge of memories played over her brain, and from out-of-the blue, seized her heart. She turned back to look at Alice, who was pacing as she listened into her phone.

Grace Allen? That was a name Lia hadn't heard or thought about for quite some time. Years, perhaps. Maybe twenty.

It couldn't be Aunt Grace. Could it?

And if Grace was still in Tuckaway Bay—then what about Zach?

TWENTY YEARS LATER

Hey there! It's Maddie aka Madeleine!

I hope you enjoyed this original story of how Lia and Zach met, and that first summer they spent together. While this is the beginning of their story, there is soooo much more to come.

I wanted to provide readers a peek into of Tuckaway Bay (for free!) in the hopes you will come to love the town, the beach, the resort, and all the people as much as I do.

You'll see this story again, embedded into the heart of the first book of the series, *Beach Therapy*—but with a lot more depth and additional perspectives!

Help others find this story! The best way is to share your honest review at your favorite bookstore, on Bookbub or Goodreads, or even on my website. I would love to see your review there!

Leave a review on Maddie's website here!

Thank you for reading!

Want to read more about Tuckaway Bay?

Scroll on for more stories!

Beach Therapy

Beach therapy, they call it, with a twist of lime.

Six women return to the same beach house in Tuckaway Bay, the same week in August, for over twenty years, drinking and laughing their past year's problems away. Beach therapy, they call it, with a twist of lime.

Lia contemplates a surprise marriage proposal from her long-term partner—one she doesn't want. Maggie questions the arrangement she made with her husband years earlier. Julia fights depression after a horrible loss. Wren worries about the legalities of her sister's business, while her twin, Willow, avoids a medical issue. And Alice? Her life is perfect. Right.

As their troubles escalate and beach week unravels, the women realize no amount of beach therapy will solve their problems this year.

Alice divulges a secret. Wren and Willow disappear. Maggie faces an impossible family situation. Julia confesses her addiction. And Lia wrestles with a twenty-year-old decision when an old summer love shows up at their beach house.

Can beach week, and their friendships, survive? Even with tequila?

Get Beach Therapy today!

The Space in Between: Julia's Story

How long will she stay in that space in between?

The day Julia Salinger admits to her girlfriends that she has a drinking problem, she vows to do something about it. Spending time in a recovery center helps. So does attending AA meetings and therapy. But the thing that saves her, day after day, is fixing breakfast for strangers.

It's routine. It gets her out of bed every morning.

While she and her husband, Mark, had dreams of operating their Old Louisville B&B together, her drinking put an end to that dream—and their marriage. And while Mark still shares in the business venture, the running of the inn is Julia's responsibility.

And all goes well, until it doesn't.

THE SPACE IN BETWEEN: JULIA'S STORY

Despite therapy, Julia wrestles with the cause of her drinking—her difficulty coping with the loss of their stillborn child, months of bourbon binges covering up her grief. But now that she's sober, grief surfaces in other ways.

Her father pressures her to return to the family law firm. A friend from AA dies of an overdose. She hears a baby crying in the attic and is certain her Victorian era home is haunted. She craves the sweet oaky taste of bourbon and caves to a night of binge drinking.

She doesn't get up to fix breakfast the next morning.

Mark gives her an ultimatum.

That's when Julia decides her best therapy is the beach, and heads to Tuckaway Bay for solace, healing, and her girlfriends. A secluded cottage at the end of the Sea Glass Inn Resort becomes her sanctuary, where she lets very few people into her life for weeks—except for the older man who surf fishes in front of her cottage every day.

Get The Space in Between today!

The Christmas Storm

They said it would be a quiet Christmas at the beach.

When a Nor'easter sweeps into the coastal town of Tuckaway Bay on Christmas Eve, the residents and guests of Sea Glass Inn prepare to hunker down and weather the storm. But which is worse—the storm raging outside, or the one brewing *inside* the inn?

Having survived their first year of running Sea Glass Inn—and a year of marriage—Zach and Lia Allen decide to celebrate the holidays by inviting their friends back to Tuckaway Bay for the Christmas holiday weekend.

Wait. Correction.

Zach reluctantly agrees. He really wants a quiet Christmas alone with Lia.

Of course, there is plenty of room at the inn for Lia's girlfriends—even though half of the rooms are closed down for deep cleaning and painting—but what about the children and significant others? Not to mention Zach's friends from New Hampshire who crash the inn after the Nor'easter cancels their winter fishing expedition.

As if space is the only issue...

Is the resort large enough to handle fluctuating family dynamics, teenage angst, pregnancy hormones, and perimenopausal women? Can Sea Glass Inn, and its guests, survive the mood swings and hot flashes?

Fa-la-la-la-la. Let the reindeer games begin!

Get The Christmas Storm today!

The Me I Left Behind: Maggie's Story

Can she find the girl she left behind on the shores of Tuckaway Bay?

When Maggie Oliver married her husband Max, she knew what she was signing on for—but did she really think through the consequences of an open marriage?

Open for Max. Not her.

That was the trade-off. Max got his kicks outside the marriage. Maggie wanted for nothing.

She had money, a big house on the golf course, private schools for the kids, and social relationships. Bonus: the sex with Max, while often rough and dominant, was fantastic.

Maggie had everything she ever wanted and was well taken care of—Max reminded her of that often. So what if he had his share of discreet dalliances?

THE ME I LEFT BEHIND: MAGGIE'S STORY

When the babies came, though, things changed. Max became less tolerant and increasingly abusive—both mentally and physically. His belittling became a thing to do in front of the kids and guests, embarrassing Maggie, and establishing his dominance over her. When they were alone, the belittling frequently turned to battering.

Maggie knows she is slowly losing herself. What happened to that carefree girl of years' past? How in hell had she lost her in the first place? And why had she allowed Max to control her—and the children—in the ways he had?

When her teenage daughter, Carol, starts stepping into similar types of unhealthy relationships with young men, Maggie knows things must change, and takes steps in that direction.

Then something tragic happens that throws all their worlds into a downward spiral. Suddenly, Maggie's path to finding herself takes an awkward, ugly turn—and the battle she thought she would fight with Max, turns into a struggle to save her family.

Get The Me I Left Behind today!

I Wish You Love: Alice's Story

Perfect Life. Perfect wife. Content husband. Adorable kid.

Alice McBain lives to ensure everyone in her life is happy. She caters to her husband. She dotes on her daughter. She mother-hens her friends. She bends over backwards for her boss —who is also her lover.

Marilyn Morgan, Alice's boss, and the Mayor of Tuckaway Bay, is gearing up for a state Senate seat run next fall. She's made it *perfectly clear* they cannot have a *perfect relationship* with each other until certain things happen. The most important of which is keeping their relationship on the down-low until after the election. She doesn't want her constituents, or her husband, to know she's having an affair with her administrative assistant-*slash*-campaign manager, until long after she's settled into her new political position at the capital.

Alice understands this—but still itches to move things forward.

After all, they've kept their long-term relationship secret for over a dozen years. Maybe it's time to come out and live that perfect life together they've so often talked about and dreamed of.

So, Alice takes some steps. Tells her own husband. Upsets her daughter. Word gets out. Her perfect life—*all their perfectly content and adorable lives*—speedily crumbles.

And there's not a damn thing Alice McBain can do about any of it.

Get I Wish You Love today!

About Madeleine Jaimes

Madeleine Jaimes is the women's fiction pen name for bestselling romance author Maddie James.

While Maddie dabbles with cowboys and small town happily-ever-afters, Madeleine explores the real-life, complicated relationships of women, men, and families, and tackles those problems through story. She figures she's lived long enough to bring some of her own life experiences into the mix.

Maddie also writes mainstream romantic suspense as M.L. Jameson.

Maddie James and pen names have published over 70 romance titles worldwide, and in a variety of formats (ebook, print, audiobook, and more). Affaire de Coeur says, "James shows a special talent for traditional romance," and RT Book Reviews claims, "James deftly combines romance and suspense, so hop on for an exhilarating ride."

Learn more at www.maddiejamesbooks.com

Made in the USA
Columbia, SC
03 June 2025